Frog and the Birdsong

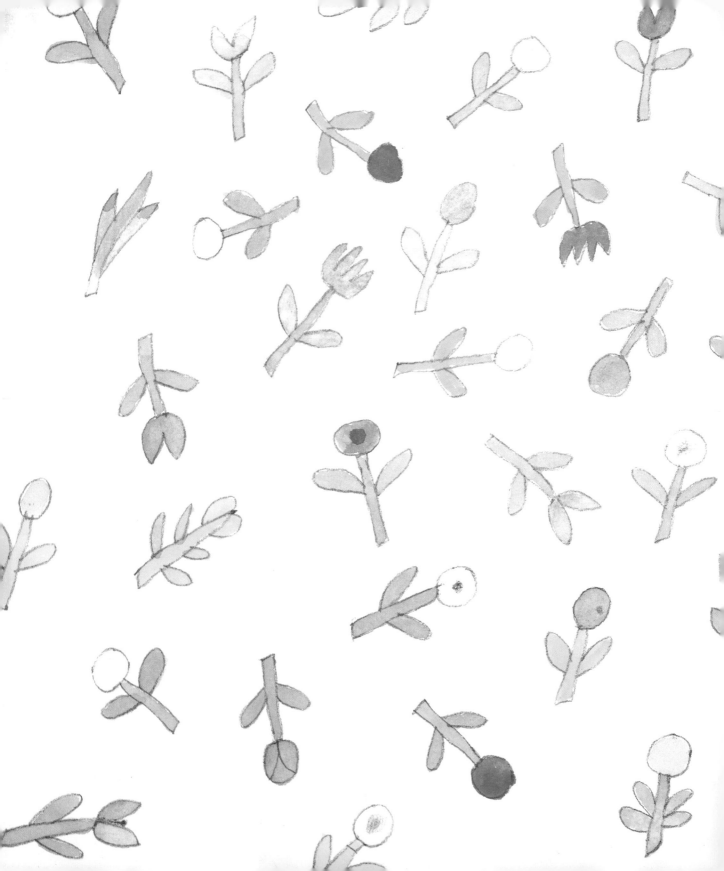

Copyright © 1991 by Max Velthuijs.
This translation copyright © 1991 by Andersen Press.
The rights of Max Velthuijs to be identified as the author and illustrator of this work have
been asserted by him in accordance with the Copyright, Designs and Patents Act, 1988.
First published in Great Britain in 1991 by Andersen Press Ltd., 20 Vauxhall Bridge Road,
London SW1V 2SA.. This paperback edition first published in 1999 by Andersen Press Ltd.
Published in Australia by Random House Australia Pty., 20 Alfred Street, Milsons Point,
Sydney, NSW 2061. All rights reserved. Colour separated in Switzerland by Photolitho AG,
Gossau, Zürich. Printed and bound in Italy by Grafiche AZ, Verona.

10   9   8   7   6   5   4   3   2   1

British Library Cataloguing in Publication Data available.

ISBN 0 86264 908 0
This book has been printed on acid-free paper

Max Velthuijs
Frog and the Birdsong

Andersen Press · London

It was a beautiful autumn day.
Pig was picking ripe apples in the orchard . . .

. . . when along came Frog. He looked worried.

"I've found something," he said.
"What is it?" asked Pig.

"Come with me and I'll show you," replied Frog.

And they set off together.
Pig felt nervous.

When they arrived at a clearing, Frog pointed at the ground. "Look," he said. "There's something wrong with this blackbird. He's not moving."

"He's asleep," said Pig.

Just then, Duck arrived.

"What's the matter?" she asked with concern.
"Has there been an accident?"
"Ssh, he's asleep," said Frog.
But Duck thought he looked ill.

At that moment Hare was walking through the woods. He saw from a distance that something was going on and joined the others.

He knelt beside the bird and said, "He's dead."
"Dead," said Frog. "What's that?"
Hare pointed up at the blue sky.

"Everything dies," he said.
"Even us?" asked Frog.
Hare wasn't sure. "Perhaps, when we're old," he said.

"We must bury him," said Hare, "over there, at the bottom
of the hill."

Together, they made a stretcher and carried the bird into the meadow.

They dug a deep hole in the ground.

"All his life he sang beautifully for us," said Hare.
"Now he has earned his rest."

Very carefully they laid the dead bird in the hole. Frog threw flowers all around it and then they covered the bird with earth.

Finally they put a beautiful stone on top. It was very peaceful. There was not a sound – not even one note of birdsong.

They were all very moved and went quietly on their way.
Suddenly, Frog ran ahead.

"Let's play catch," he shouted excitedly. "Pig, you're IT."

They played and laughed until·sunset.

"Isn't life wonderful?" said Frog.

The tired friends set off happily for home.
As they passed the bottom of the hill, they heard a sound.
There in a tree was a blackbird singing a lovely song –
as always.

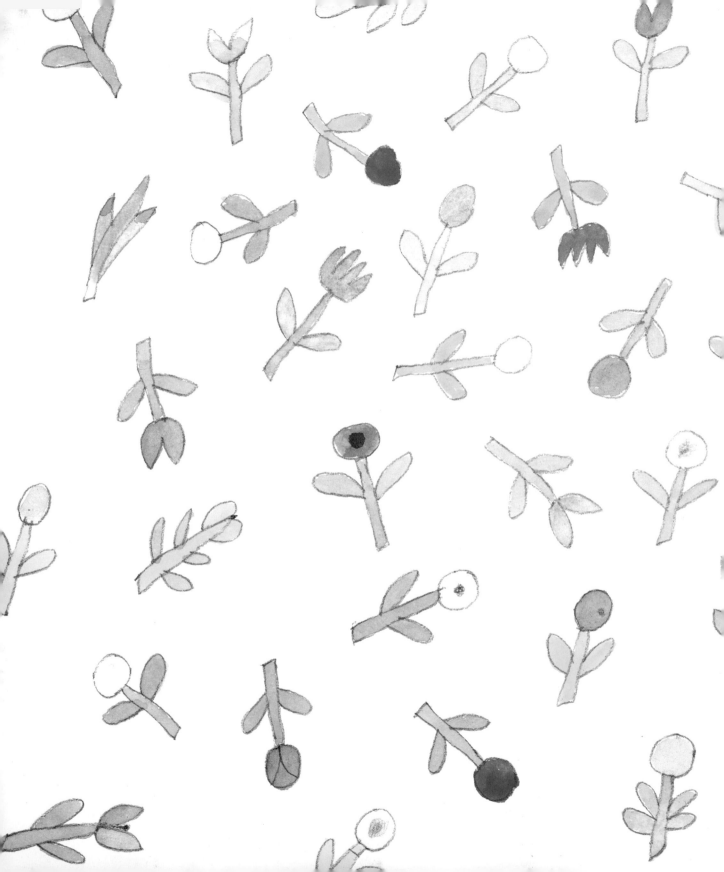